◊▽◊▽◊▽◊▽◊▽◊▽◊▽◊

Leo's world is full of **MONSTERS**, but his family, friends, and fellow villagers know nothing about that. What lies beyond the Village Wall is **TOP SECRET** and, as the **GUARDIAN'S APPRENTICE**, Leo has sworn to keep this secret safe.

Armed with a **SLINGSHOT**, pouch of **MAGICAL STONES**, and **MONSTER MAP**, it's Leo's job to keep his world in balance—protecting his village from the monsters that surround it.

◊▽◊▽◊▽◊▽◊▽◊

First American Edition 2022
Kane Miller, A Division of EDC Publishing

Text copyright © Kris Humphrey 2021
Illustrations copyright © Pete Williamson 2021
Leo's Map of Monsters: The Frightmare was originally published
in English in 2021. This edition is published by arrangement
with Oxford University Press.

For information contact:
Kane Miller, A Division of EDC Publishing
5402 S 122nd E Ave
Tulsa, OK 74146
www.kanemiller.com
www.myubam.com

Library of Congress Control Number: 2021948330

Printed and bound in the United States of America
1 2022

ISBN: 978-1-68464-487-2

LEO'S MAP OF MONSTERS

THE FRIGHTMARE

KRIS HUMPHREY

ILLUSTRATED BY

PETE WILLIAMSON

Kane Miller
A DIVISION OF EDC PUBLISHING

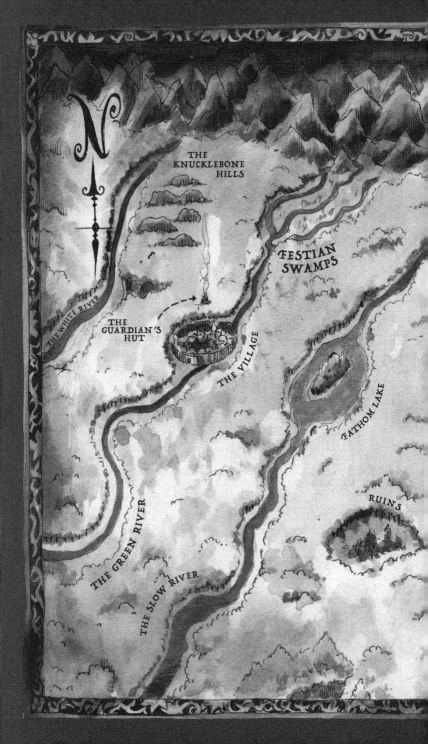

NORTHERN
MOUNTAINS

CLAY
DESERT

THE EASTERN
RIVERS

EASTERN
PLAINS

MEET THE
CHARACTERS

LEO: THE GUARDIAN'S APPRENTICE

GILDA: THE VILLAGE CHIEF

HENRIK: THE GUARDIAN

STARLA: LEO'S MONSTER FRIEND

JACOB: LEO'S BEST FRIEND

ONe

It was early evening and the walls of my bedroom were striped with shadows.

Outside, the street was busy with footsteps and excited voices. The whole village was on the move, heading toward the main square to celebrate the most exciting night of the year: Spring Festival. There would be games with prizes, food stalls, music, dancing, and a huge bonfire in the middle of the square. I couldn't wait to get down there, but first I had to find my last clean pair of socks.

I glared around my room in frustration. Then I heard my name being shouted outside.

I rushed to the window and leaned out. It was Jacob, standing with his arms folded while groups of villagers swerved around him.

"Hurry up!" he called. "We're missing everything!"

"I'm coming!" I shouted. "I just need to find some . . . oh."

My socks lay bundled on the windowsill and I remembered that I'd cleverly placed them there so that they wouldn't get lost.

A few seconds later, I was charging down the stairs, then waving to Mum as I rushed across the living room toward the door.

"Don't forget," she said, "my bit starts right after the dancing."

"Of course I won't forget!" I replied, slipping my boots on and tying the laces as quickly as I could.

Mum had helped to organize the festival's grand finale, but she'd kept it a secret from everyone, even me and my sister, Lulu. Whatever it was, I knew it was going to be great, much better than the choir of goats John the fishmonger had organized last year.

I said goodbye and stepped out onto the cobbles to meet Jacob. Then we hurried downhill toward the main square.

There were candles glowing in windows and lanterns hanging over doors. Delicious smells drifted through the streets: ginger biscuits and raisin bread, roasted chestnuts and spicy soup. We reached the bridge and crossed above the rushing curve of the river. The din of voices grew louder as we turned the corner and arrived in the bustling square, the heart of the festival.

"Look at the size of that bonfire!" Jacob said.

It was a big one, all right, and they were still adding wood to the top.

"We should get a spot right at the front for the lighting," I said.

Jacob nodded seriously and we both gazed up at the sky, checking to see how high the sun was. There would be watchers on the Village Wall, ready to signal with a drumbeat when the sun finally dropped below the Western Mountains. Then, Gilda, the Village Chief, would light the bonfire and Spring Festival would truly begin.

Of course, the food stalls were already open, and I was eager to try my first raisin bun of the night. We weaved our way through the crowds and by the time we reached the baker's stall my stomach was rumbling loudly.

Moments later, while I was sinking

my teeth into the sweet, cinnamon-flavored bread, Jacob nudged me with his elbow.

"Hey, look," he said. "Topple the Turnip. Let's have a go."

A few stalls down, there stood a brightly striped tent that was open at the front. A line of villagers stood behind a rope barrier at the opening, chucking balls into the tent and concentrating so hard it seemed their lives depended on it. As we drew nearer I saw that a row of vertical stakes had been set up at the back of the tent, each one with a fat, round turnip balanced on top. A tall, red-faced man threw a ball, missing his turnip by a long way and striking the canvas of the tent with a dull thump. Next, a young girl took a throw and grazed her turnip, making it wobble on its stake. She watched excitedly, then frowned as the turnip refused to fall.

Jacob paid the stallholder and returned with two small baskets of balls. I was still chewing on my raisin bun.

"Here you go," Jacob said, grinning. "Five goes each. If you topple a turnip you win a free snack."

We lined up at the rope barrier and placed our baskets on the ground.

"You go first," I said, taking another

bite of my bun.

Jacob took his first ball, turned sideways and squinted into the tent. He threw the ball hard and straight, but it flew over the top of the turnip.

"Just getting my aim right," he said.

Before I could gulp down my last bit of bun, he'd grabbed another ball and sent it flying. Again, it missed. All along the line, balls flew from hands and crashed into the back of the tent. A small, scared-looking boy scrambled about, collecting the balls in a large bucket and trying not to get hit.

Jacob had missed his third shot by the time I was ready to go. I felt the weight of the ball in my palm. It felt good for throwing.

I didn't think too hard, just let my eyes focus softly on the turnip at the back of the tent. I waited for Jacob to throw his final ball—and miss—then I swung my arm and watched the ball fly. It curved slightly in the air, a short, smooth arc that ended right in the center of the turnip. There was a low thud. My ball bounced up, spinning through the air. And the turnip toppled to the ground.

Jacob stared at me.

"You've got to be kidding!" he said. "First time?"

I shrugged, feeling a grin spread across my face.

The stallholder ambled over to us.

"Well done," he said, without the slightest hint of enthusiasm.

Then he thrust my prize at me: a steaming hot turnip impaled on a stick.

"You want salt and pepper?" he asked.

"Uh, no thanks," I said, taking the turnip.

"Unbelievable," Jacob muttered as the stallholder walked away.

I sniffed the turnip.

"You want this?" I asked Jacob.

He shook his head.

"You can throw the rest of mine if you like," I told him, nodding at my almost-full basket of balls.

I could see he was annoyed and that he wanted to say no, but he couldn't resist.

"Thanks," he said. "I guess I need

the practice."

I took a small bite of my turnip-on-a-stick and turned to watch the gentle bustle of villagers strolling around the square. The evening shadows were growing longer and the unlit bonfire rose above the crowds like a giant bird's nest. This was always the most exciting night of the year—the only time when everyone in the village, young or old, would stay up all night, singing, and dancing, and eating, enjoying the crackling heat of the bonfire and the warm glow of the candles and lanterns.

I saw a familiar figure moving through the crowd. It was Gilda, stopping to greet a different villager every few steps. She wore her long, deep-green cloak and carried the flaming torch she would use to light the bonfire as soon as the sun set.

Seeing Gilda reminded me how lucky I was to not be working with the Guardian tonight. Henrik had been particularly demanding lately, keeping me late each evening so he could test me on what I'd learned in his ancient books and how well I could use the Map of Monsters. But at lunchtime that day, Henrik had told me gruffly that I could take the afternoon off if I wanted it.

I took another tentative bite of my turnip, which wasn't actually all that bad, and when I looked up I saw Gilda drawing nearer to me. She was walking alongside one of the village councilors, nodding as the old man talked and talked. Gilda looked up as if she had sensed me watching. She met my gaze and I could tell right then that I wasn't going to get a night off after all.

"Good evening, Leo," she said, arriving beside me once the elderly councilor had left her in peace.

"Hi," I replied.

She was alone now, and I glanced behind me to see Jacob still concentrating hard on his turnip toppling.

"I'm afraid Henrik needs you," whispered Gilda. "Right away."

My stomach tightened. I wanted to ask if he really needed me, if maybe this time he could manage things by himself. But I knew better than that. And anyway, protecting the village was my duty. If I failed, the consequences would be disastrous.

So I took one more bite of turnip and handed the rest to Gilda.

"Careful," I said. "It's hot."

Gilda strolled away and I turned to find Jacob glaring into the turnip-toppling tent and shaking his head. He'd used up all the balls and his turnip was still standing.

"Gilda wants me to help out with something backstage," I told him. "I won't be long."

Jacob looked puzzled for a moment, then he shrugged.

"All right," he said, reaching into a pocket for some more coins. "I'll be right here. This turnip is not getting the better of me."

◂ ◊ △ ◊ ▸

As I left the main square, my mind buzzed with frustration. I was going to miss Spring Festival because of a monster. And even worse than that: I'd lied to Jacob and left him on his own. His night was ruined too, and I couldn't even tell him the real reason why.

I rushed through the empty village streets and found the turnip man's

19

house empty. In the back room, I felt for the secret latch and pulled the door open with a creak of hinges. A cool wind rushed over me and I stared for a moment, letting my eyesight adjust to the darkness. Then, I took a deep breath and stepped out into the wild.

I'd never left the village this late before and the ancient, twisted trees seemed watchful and alive. I had hurried along the path as far as the tall white stone, when I paused to look back. The forest floor was a shifting web of shadows. Every bush and tree stump took the form of a lurking monster, and for a moment I thought I'd heard footsteps. But the only sounds were the wind in the trees and my own pulse thumping in my head.

I took the narrow path up through the thorns and felt relieved to see the glowing windows of the Guardian's cabin appear between the trees.

TWo

"I didn't think you were coming," Henrik grumbled as I closed the cabin door behind me.

The Guardian's hut was brightly lit for once, with candles placed all around the cluttered room and a pair of old iron lanterns hanging from the rafters. I wondered if Henrik was celebrating the festival after all. Either that or he simply needed the extra light so he could see what he was doing.

The Guardian was standing on a chair, rummaging through the contents of one of the cabin's highest, dustiest shelves.

"I know they're in here somewhere," he muttered to himself.

"What are you looking for?" I asked.

Henrik didn't answer my question. A few moments later he made a satisfied grunt and climbed down from his chair, clutching a fist-sized glass jar. As he placed it on his desk I saw that the jar was sealed with a wide cork stopper, and the stopper had several small holes in the top.

"We've got a problem, boy," he said,
shoving the jar across the desk as I
approached.

"Let me guess," I replied. "A monster?"

He fixed me with a cold stare.

"You're half right," he growled,

bending to grab the pouch of slingshot stones from his desk drawer.

As he placed the pouch on the desk I could hear how empty it was.

"We're running low," he said. "Too many wasted shots."

I didn't really think that was fair. I was getting much better with the slingshot, practicing every day for weeks now. And tonight, I'd toppled that turnip on the first try, even without the slingshot to help me aim. I was about to tell Henrik all of this when he placed the Map of Monsters on his desk and abruptly unfolded it.

The monster lights glowed, darting and creeping all across the ancient paper. They showed the exact location and movements of all nearby monsters.

"Tell me what you know about this," Henrik said, pointing at a small green light to the west of the village.

I leaned closer. Green meant it was a forest monster. It was sort of leaf shaped and I knew I'd seen it before in one of Henrik's books.

"A Grass Gulper," I said, glancing uncertainly at the Guardian.

His brief twitch of a smile told me I was right.

"They usually stick to the meadows," I went on, "eating pretty much any green thing they can find. And they grow in size as they eat, expanding until their bellies are totally full."

"They don't like being interrupted during meals either," Henrik said. "A hungry Gulper could easily knock a hole in this wall. They may look like big, cuddly bunny rabbits, but you're going to have to be careful, lad. Those tails . . ." He shook his head. "Just make sure you spot it before it spots you, all right?"

I nodded, suddenly wishing I was back in the village square with Jacob.

Henrik's finger hovered over the Grass Gulper's light on the map.

"You see where it's heading?" he asked me.

I peered closer. At first, I'd thought it was completely still, but now I realized it was creeping along, ever so slowly.

"Toward the village," I said.

Henrik nodded.

"And here's the other thing," he said. "The only stone that'll work on a Grass Gulper is the shrink-stone, and we've only got one of them left. There'll be no second chances this time."

He tapped the lid of the jar.

"When you hit the Gulper," he said, "make sure you trap it in here quick. It'll start shrinking right away, and if you lose sight of it, even for a moment, you'll have no chance of finding it. You understand?"

I nodded once again.

"Once we've got it, we can release it somewhere far from the village before it starts to grow again. Here."

Henrik rummaged inside the pouch and slid the shrink-stone across the table. Then he folded the map and placed the slingshot on top.

"That Gulper's going to be chewing through the Village Wall before midnight unless you stop it," he said. "So you'd better make that shrink-stone count."

◂ ◊ Δ ◊ ◂

I headed east along a thin path that curved toward the river. It was still light enough to see, but Henrik had given me

a small knapsack containing
a lantern and tinderbox in
case I needed them later.

According to the map, the Grass
Gulper was moving steadily toward
the village, and my plan was to cross
the river and intercept it before it got
anywhere near the Wall. The forest
creaked and groaned, and once again
I had a feeling that someone, or
something, was watching me. I picked
up my pace, jogging every few steps,
and trying not to think about what
might be out there in the trees. Instead,
I concentrated on reaching the river as
quickly as I could.

Soon, the path widened into a familiar grassy clearing and the old wooden bridge came into view. The river rushed beneath it and I thought back to my first mission as an apprentice Guardian. This was the spot where I'd finally stopped the Armored Goretusk. As I reached the center of the bridge I felt an itch in the back of my neck and I turned sharply, convinced I'd heard something moving in the trees. I stared into the crooked shadows, but saw nothing. My heart raced and when I glanced at the map it raced even faster.

A monster was coming.

An amber light was speeding toward

me down the line of the river. I turned, but instead of taking out my slingshot, I waved at the tiny shape that was emerging from the gloom.

"Starla!" I called.

"Leo Wilder!" she replied.

Starla was a Leatherwing. She came from the desert beyond the Northern Mountains and she talked by projecting her thoughts directly into my head. We'd met on my first-ever journey into the forest and had been friends ever since.

Starla swooped down and circled around me excitedly, thrashing the air with her wings and almost sending me over the edge of the bridge.

"You're back!" she said. "It's excellent to see you, Leo Wilder!"

"It's excellent to see you, too!" I replied, grinning my widest grin as I ducked past her wings and finished crossing the bridge.

"Come on," I said. "Fly with me. We don't have much time."

"So, you pack the monsters into jars now?" Starla asked me.

"This will be the first one," I said, placing the jar back into my knapsack as I trampled through the wet mulch of the forest floor.

I'd left the path in an attempt to cut the Grass Gulper off and Starla was swooping between the branches overhead, keeping a lookout. Now and then I heard the boom of a drum or a faint cheer of voices carried on the wind from the village.

I checked the map for the leaf-shaped glow of the Grass Gulper. We were close.

Very close. I peered through the half-light trying to make out any abnormal shapes between the trees and bushes. According to the books, Grass Gulpers became incredibly quiet and still when they sensed an unknown creature approaching. They also had very tall, furry ears and I knew this Gulper would have heard us coming from a long way off. I crept through the vegetation, toward a bank of earth lined with trees.

"You think it's that way, Leo Wilder?" Starla asked me.

"Maybe," I whispered.

She hovered just above my head as I carefully climbed the bank.

I reached the top and peered out across a shadowy expanse of trees, tall grass and thorny shrubs. The Gulper had to be here somewhere. I slid the slingshot carefully from my pocket, along with my one precious shrink-stone. The grass swayed between the trees and the wind was the only sound. I scanned the forest, searching for the squat, fluffy outline of the Gulper. I thought I saw something move, a tall ear among the shadows.

"Did you see that?" I whispered to Starla.

But before she could reply, a twig snapped loudly behind me and I spun, raising my slingshot and drawing back the stone.

My mouth dropped open.

"Oh, no!" cried Starla.

She flapped high into the trees and left me standing there, my slingshot aiming right between the eyes of the intruder.

"Jacob?" I said.

I lowered my weapon.

"What are you doing here?" I asked him.

"You said you were helping Gilda," he replied, staring up into the trees as if he couldn't believe he'd just seen a flying weasel. "I thought I could help too, so I tried to catch up with you."

He looked confused and scared. This was his first time outside the Village Wall and his gaze darted about as if he was expecting to be attacked by a bear at any moment.

"What's going on?" he asked me. "You said your Assignment was forest maintenance, but this isn't forest maintenance. A secret door in the back of the turnip man's house? That flying thing you were just talking to . . . ?"

He trailed off, as if it was all too much to take in.

My mind worked furiously, searching for a way to explain what he'd seen without giving away the secrets Henrik had entrusted to me. But while I scrambled for the right words, I saw the fear in Jacob's expression intensify.

He was staring past me into the semi-dark of the forest.

I turned around slowly.

Less than ten paces away the Grass Gulper crouched in the long grass. It was bigger than I'd expected, almost as tall as me and wide enough that it would have struggled to squeeze through the front door at home. Its long ears lay flat against its back and its eyes were narrowed aggressively. It was covered all over with thick, golden-brown fur.

"Don't move," I whispered to Jacob.

I knew that any sudden sound or movement might cause the monster to attack, so I raised my slingshot as slowly as I possibly could. I only had one chance to shrink this giant rabbit down to

a safer size, and I took aim carefully, breathing deeply as Henrik had taught me, focusing on my target and not on the stone or the slingshot.

The monster's left ear twitched. It sniffed the air and opened its mouth ever so slightly to show a glimpse of its huge rectangular teeth.

I steadied my arm and breathed in, ready to fire. But from behind me, I heard a soft crunch of leaves, and the sliding of boots down the bank as Jacob tried to run away.

That was all the Grass Gulper needed.

Its ears flew up and its eyes widened, and before I knew it, there was half a ton of fur leaping toward me.

"Get down!" I shouted to Jacob as I dropped to the ground.

The Gulper flashed over me, swinging its thick tail downward and barely missing my face. I rolled and looked up and saw the creature clinging to a nearby tree trunk with its claws. I also saw Jacob sprinting away through the trees.

The Grass Gulper saw him too, and it leaped again, springing off the tree and gliding through the air.

"Look out!" I shouted.

Jacob tried to dodge out of the way, but he wasn't fast enough. The Grass Gulper struck him with its tail, so hard it lifted him off his feet and sent him crashing into the nearest tree. He grunted and fell to the ground. The Grass Gulper leapt away into the shadows.

"Jacob!" I shouted. "Are you all right?"

He didn't answer and I began to panic. What had I done, letting him follow me into the woods and get attacked by a monster?

I scanned the trees for the Gulper. It could attack again at any moment. I had to capture it fast and get Jacob some help.

I climbed to my feet, gripping my slingshot and peering into the dark tangle of branches where the monster had fled.

It was then that I realized that I'd lost the shrink-stone.

THRee

I scrambled back across the bank, searching for the stone. I could hear Jacob moving about down below, which meant he was alive at least. But without the stone, I had no way to defend us.

"Starla!" I shouted. "Where are you?"

"I'm up here, Leo Wilder," she replied. "Where is that village boy? Is he gone?"

"He's my friend," I said. "And he's

hurt. I've dropped my shrink-stone. Can you help me find it?"

I heard her wings batting the air and an instant later she was snuffling about on the forest floor beside me, sniffing out the stone with her powerful sense of smell.

"Here!" she said, pointing with her nose. "Here it is!"

"Thanks," I said, grabbing the shrink-stone and fitting it into the slingshot.

Jacob was back on his feet, staggering from side to side and clutching his left arm.

I wanted to run down there and help, but I could see better from where I was. I stared into the shadowy trees. Had the monster gone or was it watching us?

Jacob turned and looked at me. There was blood on his face and he was squinting in pain.

"What was that?" he shouted.

I shook my head and held a finger to my lips to try and keep him quiet.

Behind him, partially hidden in a tree, I'd spotted a large furry shape.

"Leo?" Jacob said, looking even more worried.

I slowed my breathing, focusing on the gold-colored ears poking out from behind the tree trunk. I drew back the stone and felt the tension build in the rubber cords. I let everything else fade into the background. And when the Gulper attacked, I was ready.

It leapt from its hiding place, directly toward Jacob.

I followed its trajectory, adjusting for speed and distance without thinking. And I let the shrink-stone fly.

As soon as the stone left the slingshot I sprinted down the bank toward Jacob.

A moment later, the stone hit the Gulper's furry body and exploded with a crackling thunderclap of energy.

Jacob cried out as the monster bore down on him, but it had already shrunk to half its original bulk. By the time it reached him it was the size of a well-fed mouse.

Jacob hopped backward as the
miniaturized Gulper landed on the forest
floor right at his feet. I arrived, swinging
my knapsack off and grabbing the jar
from inside.

"It's there!" Jacob said, pointing
downward.

The monster was twitching about in the mud. It looked confused, but didn't seem to be hurt.

I opened the jar, scooped the tiny ball of fur off the ground, and placed it carefully inside. Then, I jammed the stopper in place and checked the air holes to make sure it could breathe.

"Are you all right?" I asked Jacob.

"I'm fine," he said, clutching his arm as he stared at the miniaturized Grass Gulper in the jar.

"Hmm," I said. "Maybe we should get that arm checked out. Come on."

We started walking, back toward the bridge. Every few steps Jacob winced silently, trying to hide his pain. As well as his injured arm, there was a thin trickle of blood on the side of his face. I felt terrible for letting him follow me and even worse for letting him get hurt.

"I knew you were hiding something," he said. "Sneaking out to the forest every day. But I never thought you'd be doing . . . this."

He bent close to take a look at the Grass Gulper.

"That's not a normal animal," he said. "And that wasn't a normal slingshot you just used. I can see why you were keeping all this a secret."

The tiny monster flung itself at the

glass wall of the jar and Jacob flinched
away, laughing nervously.

"So what's your Assignment really?"
he asked. "Are you some kind of animal
hunter?"

"I'm an apprentice Guardian," I said. "My job is to stop any monsters from getting too close to the village, and to make sure the monsters stay secret."

"Monsters," Jacob repeated thoughtfully, peering out into the darkening forest.

I scanned the trees too and noticed Starla had vanished again. She didn't trust other humans and she'd be keeping her distance as long as Jacob was with me.

"Sorry you got hurt," I said to Jacob. "You weren't supposed to see any of this. And you definitely weren't supposed to get attacked."

"It's only a scratch," Jacob said, wincing

as he spoke. "And don't worry about your secret Assignment. I'm not going to tell anyone, I promise."

"I know," I said, "but Henrik's not going to like it. He's the Guardian and he's kind of strict."

"Then I'll go back to the village right now," Jacob said. "I'll tell everyone I fell off a wall or something."

I shook my head.

"He'll find out somehow," I said. "That's what he's like. We're going to have to tell him."

So I led the way, taking us back toward the cabin.

Jacob bombarded me with questions

as we walked and once I'd gotten over the fact that he was out there with me, it felt good to share what I knew about the monsters. I showed him the map and he gasped in amazement, just like I had when I'd first seen those magical lights.

Before long we were planning our adventures together. Now that Jacob knew about the monsters, Henrik would have to make him an apprentice Guardian, too. We could train together, exploring the forest and protecting the village as a team. The monsters wouldn't stand a chance.

FoUR

"No," growled Henrik. "Absolutely not."

I'd left Jacob outside so I could break the news to Henrik gently, but it hadn't made much difference. The Guardian glared at me from behind his desk. He'd extinguished all the candles and just one lantern hung from the rafters, casting ominous shadows over his craggy face.

"How could you possibly think this

was a good idea?" he demanded. "What was it, boy? You thought we didn't have enough problems already?"

"I didn't mean for it to happen," I said. "Jacob followed me. He wanted to see what I did out in the forest and then he saw the Gulper and . . ."

I trailed off as the Guardian shook his head wearily.

"Well, you've really done it this time."

He stared down at his desk for a moment, his brow creased in an angry frown. The Grass Gulper hopped about inside the jar, making it rattle against the desktop.

"So this friend of yours is injured?" he

asked me finally.

"His arm," I said. "And a cut on his head."

Henrik sighed.

"Well, you'd better get him inside then."

◄ ◊ Δ ◊ ►

I leaned against the wall, sipping the hot tea Henrik had made for us all, and watching as the Guardian tended to Jacob's arm. He worked quickly and was surprisingly gentle. After checking for pain, and seeing how easily Jacob could bend his arm at the elbow and shoulder, Henrik declared it only a "minor break." He made a sling from an old piece of fabric and examined Jacob's head in search of the cut.

"Nothing serious," he said. "But we'll need to make sure it heals properly."

He turned to me, pointing at a stack of wicker baskets.

"Grab one of those," he told me, leading the way outside to the neat little herb garden behind the cabin.

"Your friend can't be trusted," Henrik

said as soon as the door closed behind us.

"That's not true," I argued, feeling offended on Jacob's behalf. "He's a good friend and he understands how important this is. He's not going to tell anyone."

Henrik fixed me with a long, serious stare.

"Do you truly believe that, boy? I want you to think about your friend, everything you know about him. I have no doubt he's a decent lad, but that's not our concern right now. The question is: can he keep a secret this big? Is he capable of holding on to all of this and never telling another living soul?"

He raised his eyebrows at me, then

crossed to a row of short, fernlike plants at the edge of the garden.

As he crouched and carefully plucked at the leaves I considered what he'd asked me. Jacob would do everything he could to keep the monsters a secret. But would that be enough?

The more I thought about it, the less certain I became.

Jacob did have trouble keeping things to himself. Most of the village gossip I heard came from him. When he learned something interesting he got excited and then he just had to tell someone. My heart sank as I realized Henrik was right. Jacob couldn't keep a secret.

"Have you ever wondered why you were chosen as my apprentice?" Henrik asked me as he dropped a handful of leaves into my basket. "For years, Gilda's been watching you," he said. "Watching all the village children, trying to figure out who might have what it takes to become the next Guardian. You may not be much use with a slingshot, lad, but so far you've done a good job of keeping our secret safe. Gilda knew you were trustworthy. More trustworthy than Jacob, or any other child in the village. Do you understand me, boy?"

I nodded, feeling bad for Jacob but proud of myself at the same time.

"So there's only one way out of this mess," Henrik said. "We need to make sure your friend forgets everything he's seen out here in the forest."

"How?" I asked. "Do you have an herb for that?"

The Guardian let out a gruff, humorless laugh.

"I wish I did, boy," he said. "No. Herbs

won't fix this. There's only one thing that'll take your friend's memories away. We need a hair from a Frightmare's tail, and we need it tonight."

My body felt suddenly cold, and not because of the chill evening air. Frightmares were ghostly white horses with strange powers. According to Henrik's books, they haunted the high mountain passes, breathing deadly blue fire from their nostrils and guarding their territory obsessively.

"But it's almost night," I said. "And Frightmares are rock monsters. They live up in the mountains. How am I supposed to . . . ?"

"Steady on, lad," the Guardian interrupted. "They don't all live up there. A Frightmare can survive anywhere made of old stone, as long as they've got rock flowers and moss to graze on."

He stared past me as if his gaze could reach through the depths of the forest.

"The ruins," he said. "Beyond the Slow River. There's been a Frightmare haunting there for some years now. You'll have to hurry, but it's possible to get there and back in one night."

"What about Jacob?" I asked. "Is he coming too?"

"No," said Henrik. "Your friend stays with me. I'll fix the cut on his head and keep him occupied with monster stories. And I've got a blend of tea that'll make the hours he spends here seem much shorter to him. We're lucky it's Spring Festival. You won't be missed, but we'll have to get you both back home before the festival ends."

I nodded, trying to take it all in. I'd already battled one monster and now I was supposed to trek through the forest, at nighttime, and pluck a hair from the tail of an even more dangerous one.

"I need more stones," I said. "You only gave me one for the Grass Gulper."

Henrik frowned.

"We've got two stones left and you can

have them both, but you're going to have to be smart with them." He gave me a long, stern look, then headed back toward the cabin.

"Come on," he said. "We're wasting time."

◂ ◊ Δ ◊ ▸

"Sit down, lad," Henrik told Jacob as he entered the cabin's main room. "I'm going to fix that head wound. And drink your tea before it gets cold."

Henrik glanced my way and raised his eyebrows.

"I'm just going out to fetch something," I told Jacob. "But I won't be long. Then we can go back to the village together."

"Where are you going?" Jacob asked.

He looked concerned and I knew I wasn't hiding my nerves very well.

"Not far," I lied, trying to force an easy smile.

I took the almost-empty pouch of stones from Henrik's desk drawer and slipped it into my knapsack alongside the lantern and tinderbox.

"Better get going, boy," Henrik growled.

I nodded at Jacob, tied the knapsack up and headed for the door.

FIVe

I jogged along the forest path with the Map of Monsters gripped tight in my hand. The wind had grown even colder, and above the trees the sky was the deepest blue possible. The stars were out and a full moon hung low over the Northern Mountains.

The moonlight meant I could see the path in front of me, but when I dared to look sideways into the trees the view quickly blurred into a frightening mass of crooked shadows. Every time I heard a suspicious noise I checked the map just in case a monster was creeping up on me.

The path took me close to the village and as I passed within sight of the Wall I saw the flickering of flames reaching into the sky.

The festival fire was burning.

I paused for a moment, jealous of the warm, well-fed crowds in the village square. Then I pulled my collar a little tighter around my neck and set off once again.

I crossed the old wooden bridge over the Green River and took a southbound path that led toward the lower end of Fathom Lake. Tracing my route on the map, I realized that my journey to find the Frightmare would take me further from the village than I'd ever been before.

Just as I was resigning myself to this long, lonely journey, I saw an amber light dart across the map. My spirits immediately rose and I turned to watch Starla swoop toward me through the dark tunnel of trees.

"I thought you'd abandoned me," I joked.

Starla looked shocked as she hovered in front of me.

"No, Leo Wilder!" she cried. "A friend never abandons another friend. But also, a Leatherwing like me does not spend time with strange people from your village. No way."

I smiled.

"Well, I suppose that's fair," I said. "I'm just glad you're here now."

And I really was glad. The task ahead already felt a little less daunting now that Starla was with me.

But still, when I looked at the map, the ruins seemed a very long way away and the silvery-gray light of the Frightmare glowed ominously.

◄ ◊ Δ ◊ ►

As I jogged along the moonlit paths Starla flew just above me, sharing what she knew about the Frightmare.

"The ruins are the Frightmare's territory," she explained. "No other monsters go in there—not unless they are looking for trouble, Leo Wilder."

"Like we are," I said.

"Yes," she replied. "If you want a hair from a Frightmare's tail, then you must also be prepared for trouble. And your stones may not be totally useful. The Frightmare is a powerful monster. It can protect itself from magic."

"Right," I said, feeling worse and worse the more information Starla gave me.

"But there is one good thing," she went on. "This monster cannot leave its territory. We are safe until we go into the ruins, so we can find a place to watch and hide."

That didn't make me feel a whole lot better. But it did make me wonder something.

"If it can't leave the ruins," I asked, pausing for breath as I ran, "how did it get there in the first place?"

"Frightmares can roam only at particular times," Starla replied. "Only when the moon is full."

I stopped running.

"The moon's full tonight!" I said. "That monster could be anywhere!"

"Tonight is not a full moon," she replied. "Look at the sky, Leo Wilder. The moon is one day smaller than full. Even a bat could see that. It is not even close."

"Well, it looks full to me," I said, pretty sure I was right.

I shook my head and breathed slowly for a moment or two. I felt angry at all the bad luck I was getting. But being angry wouldn't help. I still had to complete the mission. If I failed, the secret would get out and the village would never be the same again. Neither would the forest.

"Come on, Leo Wilder," said Starla.

She landed on my shoulder and gave me an encouraging nudge with her nose.

I nodded, filled my lungs with the cold night air, and set off running once again.

◂ ◊ Δ ◊ ▸

We reached the Slow River and stopped for a rest. It definitely was slow, but it was wide, too, and Starla led me south along the riverbank until we reached a narrower section. The water shone in the moonlight and a line of huge rocks rose above the surface, forming a jagged chain of islands from one bank to the other.

As we grew closer I realized that the rocks were piles of crumbling brickwork all covered with moss.

"It looks like it used to be a bridge," I said.

Starla nodded.

"Very old stones, Leo Wilder."

I studied the map closely, but only when I held it up to the moonlight did the bridge become visible. It was etched so faintly that it seemed more like the ghostly outline of a bridge. I folded the map away safely and began clambering onto its half-sunken remains, leaping from one stony island to the next and doing my best not to slip on the moss.

The river flowed quietly all around me and when I made my final leap onto the opposite bank I found that the ground was hard beneath my boots.

"A road," I said, checking the map. It was drawn with the same ghostly detail as the bridge. I peered ahead into the gloom.

"It leads to the ruins," I said.

Starla swooped down and hovered beside me.

"Yes," she said. "Are you ready, Leo Wilder?"

I glanced up at the moon and felt a cold shiver run through me.

"Let's go," I said.

The road was made from flat stones laid side by side in an interlocking pattern, and long ago it must have looked very grand indeed. Now it was covered in grass and mud. Large sections had been torn apart by the growth of tree roots, and the forest had crept in on both sides, gradually swallowing it up.

Despite all this, the ancient road was easy to follow. It led us through the forest until the ruins themselves finally emerged up ahead.

The first thing I saw was a mighty stone archway standing alone over the road.

The pointed tip of the arch rose above the highest branches of the surrounding trees and its gray stone was patterned with vines and moss. As we approached, I saw walls leading away on either side. Large sections had collapsed and the parts that still stood were low, and jagged, and covered with vegetation.

I stopped before we got too close and unfolded the map.

"The Frightmare's somewhere in the middle," I said to Starla.

I noticed that its silvery light was brighter than the lights of the other rock monsters. It was star shaped, too, and I wondered if this had anything to do with the Frightmare's magic-resistant powers. Whatever the reason, that light was moving slowly away from us, near the center of the ruins.

"They like to patrol their territory," Starla said. "Always watching. Always deep inside their own big cloud of magic fog. We need to find a hiding place, Leo Wilder. Somewhere on the wall so we can wait for it to pass."

On the map, the Frightmare's monster light reached the far side of the ruins, then turned left and began following the boundary wall.

"Let's go this way," I said, also heading left.

We crept through the forest, staying close to the outside of the ruined wall. Above me, Starla searched for a good vantage point. It didn't take long for her to swoop down and find me.

"Up here," she said. "I have the perfect spot for you, Leo Wilder."

I followed her through a tangle of branches that turned out to be part of a huge fallen tree. The top of the trunk rested on a section of wall that rose almost as high as the archway. There were battlements lining the top and what looked like a tower of some sort just behind it.

I began climbing the steeply angled trunk, using my hands for extra grip and trying not to look down as the forest floor dropped away beneath me. When I reached the top, I carefully stepped between the battlements and down onto a high walkway.

Starla was perching there, waiting.

"What do you think, Leo Wilder?" she asked me. "Have you ever seen ruins as ruinous as these?"

I stared in disbelief.

From the map, I'd expected a small castle or maybe a very big house, but what I saw was more like a town—a whole town built from huge stone blocks

that had been abandoned and left to crumble in the middle of the forest. In the center stood four circular towers. Only one still stood at its full height, which was twice as tall as the entry arch. All four of the towers were covered with windows and balconies. Other smaller towers rose above the forest, along with isolated sections of wall, roofless buildings of all shapes, and staircases that led to nowhere.

Every part of the ruined town had been touched by the living forest. Moss and vines clung to the walls. New trees had sprouted where streets and squares used to be. The insides of houses had become wild, overgrown gardens.

"Can you see the fog, Leo Wilder?" Starla asked me, pointing with her nose.

I peered toward the northern edge of the ruins. At first, there was nothing but darkness between the trees. Then, I saw a strange swirling of air. Tendrils of fog rose from the forest floor, billowing over the tumbledown walls and forking around the branches of the trees. The fog was moving toward us, staying close to the boundary wall, and it glowed with a faint blue light.

I took out the map and saw the silver star moving steadily toward us. The Frightmare was coming.

SIX

I crouched beside Starla on the walkway and emptied the pouch of stones into my hand.

One vine-stone and one sleep-stone. That was it.

"I need a good place to shoot from," I said to Starla. "Can you help me find one?"

"Of course, Leo Wilder!" she said, flapping into the air.

I loaded the sleep-stone into the slingshot, figuring that the hair-plucking procedure would be a lot safer if the Frightmare was asleep.

"This way!" called Starla. "I've found the place for you. But quick—the fog is coming!"

She was right. The fog had begun to creep up onto the high outer wall and a blue haze was settling over everything.

I made my way along the mossy, moonlit surface and looked down to where Starla was perching. At the base of a short, steep staircase, about halfway down the wall, she had found a ledge that overlooked the street. I climbed down carefully and watched the blue fog roll through the space between the ruined buildings.

There was a vine-covered wall opposite us, which had partially collapsed, creating a huge pile of rubble. A tree had grown crookedly nearby, and it stood close enough to give us a small amount of cover. I took up a position between the branches of the tree and aimed the slingshot down into the street.

Starla crouched beside me, her amber eyes squinting into the rolling fog.

"Do you hear that, Leo Wilder?" she asked.

"Hooves," I said.

They struck the flagstones in a slow, deliberate rhythm. This was good. If the monster was patrolling its territory slowly, I had a much better chance of hitting it the first time. I tightened my grip on the slingshot, hoping the Frightmare would be visible enough inside its cloud of fog.

As it happened, I didn't have to worry about that.

I gasped as the Frightmare strode into view. It was huge, at least a pace taller than the biggest horse in the village. Its muscular body was ghostly white, and its mane and tail were a brilliant blue, rippling in a nonexistent breeze and shining like the flames of some strange, ice-cold fire.

It took me a moment to gather my wits, and by the time I'd adjusted my aim the Frightmare was almost level with us, striding up the pile of rubble with its head held high.

I narrowed my gaze, aimed down toward the horse's snow-white body, and loosed the sleep-stone.

In the fraction of a breath it took for the stone to leave the slingshot, the Frightmare turned its head. Its sharp blue eyes met mine and its nostrils flared.

The sleep-stone flew down into the street and I held my breath.

Starla was perfectly still beside me.

My shot was good. I could see the stone

curving just as I'd planned it and I allowed myself a smile. I'd done it.

But the moment before the stone hit, something very odd happened.

The Frightmare shook its billowing mane and its whole body became a blur of shining blue. Then the monster wasn't there anymore.

No hooves clattering over the rubble.

No graceful leap to safety.

The Frightmare was simply gone, and the sleep-stone sailed through the air where the ghostly horse had been, exploding in a harmless puff of dark-blue liquid against the ground.

I looked at Starla and Starla looked at me.

"Well that was not what I expected, Leo Wilder," she said.

SEVEN

I climbed down the tree and dropped onto the street. The fog was gone, and so was the Frightmare.

"How am I supposed to hit something that can disappear whenever it feels like it?" I said, examining the map in frustration.

"I told you this horse monster was powerful," Starla said, hovering high above me.

"Well, it's a shame you didn't mention that particular power," I replied.

On the map, the Frightmare's silver star stayed unmoving in the center of the ruins.

"I think it's hiding," I said. "Or waiting for us. Either way, we have to get to those central towers and find it."

"I'm not sure about this, Leo Wilder," said Starla. "Why don't we stay near the edge, near the forest, where it's safe?"

I shook my head.

"We have to go deeper into the ruins," I said, "or we'll never get that tail hair. It's all right if you want to wait here. I've got the map. I can find the Frightmare."

Starla squeezed her eyes shut for a moment. I could see she was scared. Even with her flying skills, she'd be in danger if she got too close to the Frightmare. It could breathe fire, after all.

Starla shook her head and peered out across the ruined town.

"I suppose I should come along," she said. "Just to keep you company."

I smiled and we set off together down the abandoned street.

In one hand I held the map, squinting through the moonlight to plot a course through the ruins. In the other hand, I gripped the slingshot and the final stone.

The air was damp, cold, and eerily quiet. It was hard to imagine people ever living in such a place.

"Why do you think the town was abandoned?" I asked Starla.

"People are strange," she replied, swooping down to fly closer beside me. "Very strange. And sometimes they are also stupid. No offense, Leo Wilder."

"None taken," I said, frowning.

I wound between piles of rubble, ducked through ancient doorways, and clambered over tree roots. According to the map, the Frightmare hadn't moved. I knew my only chance to hit it with the vine-stone was to sneak up without being seen. Luckily, there were plenty of things to hide behind, and we approached the central towers quietly, without ever leaving the shadows.

Soon we reached the center.

I peered out from a moss-encrusted alleyway and saw that the four tall circular towers formed the corners of a huge castle that dominated a central square. The square itself had become part of the forest, with short, gnarled trees filling all the open space. Through the trees I spotted the castle's main doorway, swirling with the Frightmare's blue fog.

"We have to be quiet," I whispered

to Starla. "If the Frightmare knows we're here it might disappear again."

"Don't worry, Leo Wilder," Starla replied. "I am actually a very quiet monster."

I wasn't sure I agreed with that. Starla usually made quite a lot of noise with her big leathery wings, but as we made our way toward the castle all I could hear was the wind through the trees and my own soft footsteps.

I drew my slingshot as we approached the entrance. The vine-stone was ready to fire and I stared into the fog, waiting for the Frightmare's glowing tail and mane to appear. I walked carefully over the mossy, uneven flagstones, weaving through the trees until I was standing directly in front of the wide, arched doorway.

There was a darker patch of blue somewhere inside, but the fog was too thick to make anything out. Starla landed on a nearby branch and I glanced up at her, nodding toward the door to suggest that we'd have to go inside.

Starla nodded back nervously and I stepped toward the door.

The fog was suddenly much thicker. The trees around me were swallowed up in the blue haze and I could barely make out the edges of the doorway. I aimed my slingshot straight ahead and stared into the fog with wide eyes.

At first, all I heard was the slow clop of the Frightmare's hooves. Then the blue light intensified, and the hoofbeats began to speed up. I stopped moving and held my slingshot steady. My heart beat hard, echoing the monstrous hoofbeats that sped toward me.

The Frightmare emerged in a burst of fog, its wild blue mane streaming. And it was charging right at me.

I loosed the vine-stone at the charging monster and dived out of the way. As I rolled, I saw blue flame erupt from the Frightmare's nose and the vine-stone vanished in a puff of smoke before it could hit its target. The Frightmare skidded to a halt and turned to face me.

I scrambled up, wondering if I could make it to the forest if I ran. But it was way too far. And I wasn't even sure if the forest would be safe.

"Into the castle!" Starla cried.

I swerved toward the doorway and found her hovering there in the fog.

"Quick," she said. "Go left and climb up high."

I did what Starla said, and found myself in a wide rubble-strewn hall. Shafts of moonlight shot through the fog, and I saw doorways leading into darkness, and narrow, open staircases that climbed the walls toward crumbling balconies and more dark doorways.

"Go up!" Starla insisted.

I sprinted for the nearest staircase and started climbing as the Frightmare's hooves clattered into the hall. The fog grew thick and the blue light was strong and disorienting. As I climbed the slippery old stairs I realized Starla was right. They were too narrow for a horse of that size.

I climbed until I reached a balcony

about ten paces up. Below me, the Frightmare reared up onto its hind legs and let out a terrifying blast of blue flame that made the wall beneath me crackle and smoke. I backed away from the edge of the balcony as an intense wave of heat rushed upward.

"This way," Starla said, swooping past me into the fog.

I turned and followed her through a low doorway that led into a corridor.

"Wait!" I called to Starla. "It's pitch-black. I can't see a thing!"

The glowing fog was gone, but I wondered if the Frightmare would be able to make itself appear in the corridor. If it did, I'd have no way to escape. It would burn me to a crisp or trample me down.

I stopped, remembering the lantern Henrik had given me. Undoing my knapsack, I thought about the Guardian back in his cabin, and Jacob patiently listening to the old man's stories. I felt a brief flash of annoyance at Jacob for following me into the forest. Then I felt instantly ashamed. Jacob couldn't help being curious. It was my fault for not checking if I was being followed. I'd landed my friend in this situation, and now here I was, trying to steal a horse hair that would erase his memory. With no stones left, it seemed unlikely I'd be doing anything of the sort. I didn't know what Henrik would do if I returned empty-handed. Maybe he'd banish me and Jacob into the forest. He definitely wouldn't let Jacob go home knowing the secret of the monsters.

I fumbled the tinderbox open and began trying to light the lantern.

Maybe banishment wouldn't be so bad? The forest wasn't all that scary and I wouldn't have to keep things secret from Jacob anymore . . .

But I knew I was being ridiculous.

Failure just wasn't an option. I had to get that magic tail hair.

"What are you doing, Leo Wilder?" Starla asked me.

I felt her land beside me in the darkness, her wing brushing up against me as I struck the flint over and over again.

"I can't see in the dark like you," I replied. "There could be holes in the floor. I could walk off the end of a wall. I have to be able to see."

Starla jumped back as the sparks caught the tinder and a flame ignited. A pool of soft yellow light bloomed around us and I rose to my feet, holding the lantern out in front of me. The corridor was narrow and the ceiling was low, which meant we were safe from the Frightmare, at least for now.

"I think we made it angry," I said to Starla.

I could hear it charging about back in the hall.

"Well, you did sneak into its home and shoot stones at it," Starla reminded me.

"They were my only two stones," I said. "Now we're stuck in this corridor and I've got nothing to defend myself with."

"I can help us get out, Leo Wilder. It would be better if you had some wings, but this ruin is big and there are lots of secret small ways you can walk in, too small for a Frightmare."

I peered back down the corridor and listened as the Frightmare let out a furious whinny and stamped its powerful hooves. Escaping felt like a great idea, but I couldn't go home without that magic tail hair.

"We can't leave," I said. "Not yet. We have to try again."

"But you have no stones, Leo Wilder! The slingshot is no use now!"

"Then we'll have to think of something else," I said.

◂ ◊ △ ◊ ▸

After creeping my way through all the darkest, smelliest, and narrowest parts of the castle, I arrived back outside. I'd given Starla the lantern and she'd flown off, swooping about in the grand hall until the Frightmare had chased her out into the streets. Hopefully, she'd be able to lead it to me. My job was to hide somewhere at ground level and I was busy squashing myself inside a hollow tree somewhere between the castle and the archway we'd seen as we'd first arrived at the ruins. The hollow was so small that I had to kneel on the damp ground, and every time I moved, my head scraped against moldy wood. All I had to do was wait for Starla to show up.

Luckily, I didn't have to wait long.

On the map, I saw Starla's amber dot racing toward me through the ruins, and moments later her voice echoed in my head.

"Where are you, Leo Wilder?"

"Here," I whispered, waving a hand outside the hollow.

"I see you, I see you!" she cried.

I took a final look at the map before folding it away. The Frightmare was on its way.

"The horse is nice and angry," Starla said, hovering in front of my tree. "You'd better run quicker than you usually run, Leo Wilder, once you've plucked its tail hair."

"I'm planning to," I replied, adjusting my position inside the hollow.

The archway and the edge of the ruins were about forty paces away. Starla had insisted that tonight was not a full moon, which meant the Frightmare wouldn't be able to follow me out into the forest. All I could do was hope that she was right.

"Get ready, Leo Wilder," she said.

The lantern light stopped moving and I could tell that Starla was getting ready to dodge the Frightmare. I knelt, ready to reach out and pluck the magic tail hair. My muscles tensed in anticipation. I felt scared. Suddenly our plan seemed ridiculously dangerous. I wanted to call out to Starla, telling her to fly for the forest so we could both escape right now.

But it was too late. The blue fog was swirling through the trees. The Frightmare had arrived.

Hooves pounded and the lantern light dimmed as Starla flapped away to avoid the charging monster. From my hiding place, I saw a blur of white and blue through the fog. Then the lantern light swept back toward me and swung from side to side.

The Frightmare stomped into view. Its hooves were so close that I could hear them grind against the moss-covered flagstones. With a terrifying whinny, the monster reared up. I heard the crackling rush of flames and hoped that Starla was high enough to avoid them. The Frightmare shifted position, rearing up again, but this time my view was filled with the brilliant blue light of its billowing tail.

I reached out of the hollow. The monster's tail was much too thick to grab just one hair, so I took hold of a small handful and I pulled.

The Frightmare spun around as the hair came free in my hand.

Its front hooves hit the ground and it tossed its head, snorting deadly blue fire in every direction.

I cowered back inside the hollow tree as flame licked the ground outside. In my hand, the lock of ghostly blue tail hair glowed brightly. I had what I'd come for, but now I was trapped.

Flames crackled against the bark of the tree and I felt the whole thing shudder as the Frightmare threw its weight against it. I stuffed the tail hairs into my pocket and pushed myself as far back into the hollow as I could. The Frightmare rammed the tree and sprayed blue fire across the opening of the hollow, turning the dead leaves at my feet into ash and singeing the toes of my boots. I pulled my feet in closer to my body, certain all of a sudden that hiding in a tree had been a terrible idea.

The tree shuddered once again, then
a screeching noise interrupted the
Frightmare's furious snorting. I saw
lantern light swing close across the
base of the
tree.

More high-pitched screeching followed and I realized what it was: Starla was trying to drive the Frightmare away.

The monster's attack on the tree seemed to stop. I saw a flash of blue and white outside and heard the thump of hooves. Blue flames crackled, but they were further away now.

"Go, Leo Wilder!" Starla cried at me. "Go to the archway, now!"

I scrambled out of the hollow and emerged into thick blue fog. Ash drifted in the air and the Frightmare was nowhere to be seen. Somewhere high up over the trees I saw lantern light swaying.

I spun around, trying to decide which way I should run. The fog was so thick that I couldn't tell where I was. It was the approaching sound of hooves that made my mind up for me.

I turned and sprinted through the trees, dodging left and right as their dark twisted shapes lurched out of the fog at me. I saw a fragment of wall, a pile of rubble, but I didn't know if I was running toward the archway or deeper into the ruins. The Frightmare was getting closer, its hooves rising to a thunderous noise that filled me with panic.

Then the yellow glow of the lantern swept over me.

"Hurry, Leo Wilder!" Starla urged. "Follow me!"

I swerved to the right and ducked beneath the branches of a stunted tree. Starla led the way, illuminating the treacherous ground with the lantern. I jumped over tree roots and broken flagstones, and skidded through patches of leaf mulch. And all the time the fog grew thicker and brighter as the Frightmare gained on me.

I glanced behind me and saw its flowing mane and furious eyes. Only the trees were keeping it from galloping at full speed and running me down.

"How far to the arch?" I shouted to

Starla.

"Not far! Not far!" she cried. "We're almost there!"

I glanced behind me once more. The monster was twenty paces away, fifteen now. It was gaining fast.

As I turned back around, my foot hit something solid and my balance was thrown completely. I stumbled onward for a few chaotic steps, then slammed into the ground. All the air was forced from my lungs.

I rolled onto my back and gasped for breath. The Frightmare clattered to a halt and loomed over me, just a few paces away. It stared down at me with its nostrils flaring, ready to burn me to ash. I scrambled backward, rising clumsily to my feet, but the monster didn't come any closer. There was no point in running. I knew I couldn't escape its vengeance now.

Suddenly the lantern appeared beside me and Starla was there.

"Go!" I told her. "Get out of here. It'll kill us both!"

"I think I'll stay here with you, Leo Wilder," she said.

I stared at her in disbelief, then back at the Frightmare. The monster reared up onto its hind legs, let out a piercing whinny, and breathed its crackling blue fire right at us.

I covered my face with my arm and tried to push Starla behind me, but the heat of the flames didn't reach us.

When I lowered my arm I saw the blue fire curling upward, as if it had struck an invisible wall about two paces ahead of me. The Frightmare snorted and scraped its hooves. It sent another blast of fire from its nostrils, and again it was deflected away.

"Look where you are, Leo Wilder,"
Starla said.

She flew above me, casting lantern
light over a section of tumbledown wall.
Higher up, I saw the grand curve of an
arch emerge from the fog.

We'd made it. The boundary of the ruins stood between us and the Frightmare.

"I guess it's not a full moon, then," I gasped, watching the Frightmare stomp and snort in frustration, breathing its blue fire against the invisible wall.

Starla descended with the lantern, shaking her head at me.

"You should know by now, Leo Wilder, that I am always right about everything."

EIGHT

It felt good to be out of the ruins and traveling away from the Frightmare's territory. Even the endless dark of the forest felt relatively safe now.

I walked fast, back along the forgotten roads and overgrown paths that had brought us to the ruins in the first place. Starla flew just ahead of me, gliding through the night air and flapping her wings lazily only when she had to. It had been a long night and we were both tired.

I thought of the strands of glowing blue hair in my pocket and I couldn't help feeling sorry for the Frightmare. We'd sneaked into its home and pulled out its hair. I definitely wouldn't like it if someone did that to me, even if they'd done it for a good reason.

It was still dark when we reached the bridge over the Green River, but I knew we wouldn't have long before Spring Festival ended with Mum's grand finale. I had to get Jacob back to the village before then. If I didn't, our parents would know something had happened.

I hurried over the old wooden bridge, finding a bit of extra strength in my legs now that I was so close to home.

Starla swooped down and flew beside me as I pressed on into the woods.

"That grumpy old Guardian should be pleased for once, Leo Wilder," she said. "You went a long way to collect those horse hairs."

"We both did," I said. "There's no way I could have done it without you."

Starla smiled at me, showing her sharp little teeth.

"You were really brave tonight," I said. "And you were right about the full moon."

"We make a good team, Leo Wilder," she said.

We arrived at the tall white stone that marked the path to Henrik's cabin.

"Time to fly," Starla said, rising up through the dark branches above us. "See you next time, Leo Wilder!"

I waved to Starla as she flapped out of sight. Then I made my way carefully into the thorn thicket.

The cabin windows glowed softly, and as I pushed open the door I caught Henrik halfway through a story.

" . . . and what do you think happened then, lad?" the Guardian said.

Jacob was sitting in Henrik's chair, his arm in a sling and a rapt expression on his face.

"Uh . . . I don't know," he replied. "Did the Vampire Slug crawl back into the cave?"

Henrik shook his head and let out a short, growling laugh.

"No it did not," he said. "It . . . "

He stopped as I walked in, his expression growing suddenly serious.

I gave him a quick nod and his face relaxed just a little.

"We'll finish that story another time," he said to Jacob. "My throat's dry. It needs more tea."

Jacob smiled at me as if he'd had the

most entertaining night of his life.

"You wouldn't believe some of the things the Guardian's been telling me," he said. "Or maybe you would. I guess all this stuff's happened to you, too? Getting chased by giant monsters? Traveling around the forest on secret missions? I asked if I could join, get trained as a Guardian like you are, and Henrik said that maybe I could. Wouldn't that be the best?"

I glanced across at Henrik, who shot me a deadly look. He was measuring some kind of powder onto a scale in the corner of the room. "That would be amazing," I said to Jacob, forcing a smile to hide my sudden sadness. If only he could train as a Guardian alongside me. If only Henrik trusted him enough.

"Would you help me in the kitchen, Leo?" the Guardian asked me.

I followed him through into the next room, feeling like I was about to betray my best friend.

"Where is it?" Henrik whispered.

I took the small bundle of Frightmare hair from my pocket and handed it over. Henrik's face shone blue as he examined it closely. He nodded.

"Well done, boy," he said.

On the small kitchen table, he extracted a single hair from the bunch and placed it into a metal tankard. Next,

he poured in some boiling water from
a kettle he had heating on the stove. He
stirred it with a metal spoon, then took
the powder he'd just measured out and
poured that into the mix. There was
a bright flash of blue and the tankard
fizzed violently for a moment.

Henrik let it settle, then he sniffed the vapor rising from the mixture, added a drop more powder and poured the whole thing into one of his small clay drinking bowls.

He quickly poured two bowls of ginger tea and added a dash of honey to all three drinks. Then he ushered me back into the main room of the cabin.

I stared into my tea, unable to watch as Jacob drank the forgetting potion. He had no idea this would erase all the wondrous things he'd seen and heard. It would erase his dream of joining me as an apprentice Guardian, too. Tomorrow he'd return to his Assignment at the Records Office,

the Assignment I'd always thought I'd
wanted. And I'd return to my old ways,
keeping everything I did a secret from my
best friend.

"How's the tea?" Henrik asked him.

Jacob took another long sip. He nodded
and opened his mouth to reply, but all
that came out was a mumbled slur. He
blinked at Henrik, then at me. Then he
slumped forward onto the desk, spilling
what was left in his bowl.

I ran to help, lifting him up by his
shoulders.

"Jacob?" I said. "Jacob?"

"He's fine," said Henrik. "In a minute
or two he'll be able to walk, a few minutes

after that he'll start to register where he is, so we have to get him to the Village Wall before that happens."

Together, we carried Jacob through the thorn thicket and along the narrow path that led to the village. We agreed on a cover story as we walked, something I could tell Jacob when he came round. As we neared the Wall, I felt him begin to stir. He coughed and twitched his head.

"Sit him down here," Henrik said.

We lowered Jacob onto a fallen tree trunk, still holding him by the shoulders until he could sit upright by himself. At that point, Henrik left us.

"Take him in through the East Gate," the Guardian told me as he stalked back toward his cabin. "Gilda's made sure there are no guards there tonight. And make sure you get the cover story right."

I nodded, watching Jacob closely. As Henrik had predicted, he began returning to his normal self a few minutes later.

"Where are we?" he asked, rubbing his head, and then wincing in pain as he tried to move his broken arm.

Before I could answer he saw the Village Wall and realized which side of it we were on.

"No way!" he cried. "How did we get

out here? And what happened to my arm? It hurts like mad."

"I had to finish up some forest maintenance and you followed me out here," I said. "You fell into a ditch and hit your head—also, I think your arm's broken."

"Hmm," he examined his arm, then looked around nervously. "Does anyone know I'm here?" he asked.

"Just me," I said. "Don't worry, I won't tell anyone."

Jacob stood up and peered into the darkness of the trees. Music drifted to us from the village and I could tell from the slow rhythm that the festival was winding down. It would soon be over.

"We should get back inside the Wall," I said, noticing the look of awe on Jacob's face as if he couldn't believe where he was.

"This is amazing," he said, reluctantly following me as I led him toward the East Gate.

◂ ◊ Δ ◊ ◂

Back in the square, we found the bonfire burning low. Most of the villagers had taken to the benches around the edge, but a few were still dancing. On the stage, the village band was plodding through a slow tune on their fiddles and drums. I saw Mum off to the side, talking to Gilda. A short while later they were joined by a man wearing a blue hooded smock that reached to his ankles and was decorated with swirling gold patterns.

"I wonder what the grand finale is going to be," Jacob said.

"I don't know," I replied. "Mum wouldn't tell me."

The stranger began to rummage in a large sack. Mum was talking to Gilda and gesturing toward the village band.

"We need a cover story," Jacob said to me.

"A what?" I asked, taken by surprise.

"For my arm," he said. "So no one knows I left the village. I'd get in so much trouble with my dad."

I'd been so caught up with lying to Jacob that I'd forgotten we'd both have to lie to everyone else as well. Sometimes it felt as if all I did was lie, but sitting there among the villagers and with my best friend beside me, I knew that the secrets I kept were important. I looked at the familiar faces all around me. If any one of them found out about the monsters, there would be panic. Village life would be turned upside down. The bravest villagers would venture out into the forest and some would venture out as hunters. People would get hurt. Monsters would get hurt. The lies I told kept the villagers safe and kept the forest and its creatures safe, too.

"We could say you fell out of a window?" I suggested to Jacob.

He laughed.

"Or I got kicked by a goat?" he replied.

"Or you slipped on some dung?"

"Or I broke my arm wrestling a pig?"

"Or picking your nose?"

We found a bench with a good view of the stage and the bonfire, and we sat down. A few moments later the band stopped playing and it was time for the grand finale. I saw Mum standing beside the stage with a serious expression on her face. She was peering out across the square, slowly scanning its edges. She nodded to someone I couldn't see. Then she nodded again, and again, all in different directions. I couldn't see the stranger in the blue smock anywhere.

Then, without any warning, a single drumbeat boomed from the stage and the square was plunged into darkness as every lantern and candle was extinguished at once. Even the bonfire seemed to vanish, although I could still hear it crackling in the center of the square.

There were gasps of surprise from the crowd, then the square fell into an expectant silence. Another drumbeat boomed from the stage and the next thing I heard was my mum's voice, clear and strong through the cool night air:

"Dear friends," she exclaimed, "to

celebrate the coming of a new spring, I present to you a traveler from afar, a man who has braved the wild wolves and bears and bandits of the forest. Please welcome to our village . . . Rhinek the Fire Mage."

The villagers clapped and cheered as the hooded man appeared beside the darkened bonfire, lit by a single flame that seemed to flicker in the palm of his hand. The Fire Mage stood there, unmoving, until the applause faded out, then a drumroll thundered from the stage and he cast the tiny flame away from him with a dramatic flourish.

The whole village gasped as the

bonfire raged back into life, reaching higher into the night sky than ever before. Suddenly the flames changed to a luminous green, with colored sparks

cascading down in spirals, sputtering out in midair.

"No way!" Jacob whispered beside me.

I watched with my mouth hanging open as the bonfire fizzed and twisted. The hooded stranger strode into view, casting handfuls of powder, changing the bonfire from green, to red, to purple, and sending spears of colored flame into the sky. Each new display was joined by a dramatic flurry of drumming from the stage.

◂ ◊ Δ ◊ ▸

A fireball flew up and exploded into a thousand glittering white stars. Then, the flames turned black once again, covering the square in darkness. The black flames crackled away and the onlookers murmured their approval. Next, with a startling pop, the fire shot up into the sky, a brilliant blue that reminded me of the Frightmare's ghostly mane.

It was in that instant that I caught a glimpse of the Fire Mage's face. My heart leapt with the shock of recognition.

From beneath his hood, Henrik's lips curled ever so slightly, smiling at me before he turned and cast another handful of powder onto the flames.

THE GRASS GULPER

STRENGTH	6	MONSTER TYPE
SIZE	2-6	Forest Monster
SPEED	8	HABITAT
INTELLIGENCE	5	Meadows and woodlands
WEAPONRY	6	DIET
		Anything green

DESCRIPTION

A furry, rabbit-like creature that grows in size as it eats. A Grass Gulper with a full belly can be as large as a bear – and just as dangerous. Their big front teeth can tear any kind of vegetation from the ground, and their tall ears make them impossible to surprise. They can leap high into the air and cling to the trunks and branches of trees with their sharp claws.

ATTACK STYLE

Grass Gulpers hate to be interrupted while they eat and will attack without warning, springing with their strong back legs, and swiping knockout blows with their thick, furry tails.

STRENGTH	7
SIZE	7
SPEED	9
INTELLIGENCE	9
WEAPONRY	9

MONSTER TYPE
Rock Monster

HABITAT
Mountains / ruins

DIET
Rock flowers and moss

DESCRIPTION

A huge, ghostly-white horse with a brilliant-blue mane and tail. Frightmares live alone, mostly haunting the high mountain passes, but they can survive anywhere made of ancient stone. They guard their territory obsessively and can only leave it during a full moon. Frightmares can protect themselves from magic and are rumored to have magical powers of their own.

ATTACK STYLE

Emerging from a haze of magic blue fog, the Frightmare charges its enemies and breathes deadly blue fire from its nostrils. It will stop at nothing to drive intruders from its territory.

THE STONES

STINK-STONE

FIRE-STONE

SLEEP-STONE

VANISH-STONE

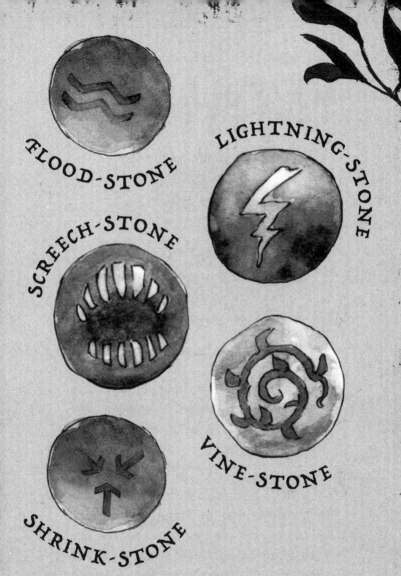

FLOOD-STONE

LIGHTNING-STONE

SCREECH-STONE

VINE-STONE

SHRINK-STONE

CHOOSE YOUR STONES WISELY . . .

KRIS HUMPHREY

Kris has done his fair share of interesting jobs (cinema projectionist, blood factory technician, bookseller, teacher). But he's always been writing—or at least thinking about writing.

In 2012 Kris graduated with distinction from the MA in Writing for Young People at Bath Spa University, winning the award for Most Promising Writer. He is the author of two series of books for young readers: *Guardians of the Wild* and now, *Leo's Map of Monsters*.

PETE WILLIAMSON

Pete is a London-based writer, illustrator, and animation designer, who has illustrated over 65 books including *Stitch Head* and *Skeleton Keys: The Unimaginary Friend*.

Read all of Leo's incredible adventures!